Fighting with Honor

A Men of Honor Novella

K.C. LYNN

Published by K.C. Lynn

Fighting with Honor Copyright © 2017 K.C. LYNN
Print Edition

First Edition: 2017

Editing: Wild Rose Editing
Formatting: BB eBooks
Cover Art by: Cover to Cover Designs

Dedication

Dedicated to my Ladies of Honor. Your unwavering support, loyalty, and love for these characters never cease to amaze me. I love our group and cherish each day we spend together. Thank you for sharing this journey with me.

Here are more Men of Honor for you.

Quick note from the author

Although the content in this story does indeed occur in real life, please note that this story is purely fictional. It has been conjured up from my imagination and is not meant to offend but merely give a *happily ever after* that we don't always get in real life.

PROLOGUE

Jaxson

Once a man pledges his honor to his country, that sacrifice is embedded in his soul forever. For years he's trained to fight, kill, and do whatever necessary to protect his country and its freedom, even if it means giving his own life.

He becomes more of a machine than human—one that's built to destroy the enemy.

When it's time to turn in his weapons, he never forgets the skills he learned. Never forgets the smell of death or feel of a rifle in his hands. The same hands that one day cradle his baby girl and caress the skin of his beautiful wife.

If anything or anyone ever tried to steal away the family he has vowed to love and protect, may God have mercy on their soul.

CHAPTER ONE

Jaxson

The early morning sun continues to rise, lighting the trail I destroy beneath my feet. Sweat coats my skin, trickling down my bare back as my lungs rage for air.

I push myself harder, relishing in the burn.

Every day I run this trail in the solitude of my property, land that I share with men who I consider brothers. Together, we fought alongside each other for our country, now we fight to protect the people we love most.

Once my house comes into view, I slow to a jog and climb up the porch steps, grabbing the newspaper that lays before the door. Walking inside, I hit the code for the alarm then head upstairs and grab a towel from the linen closet to wipe down with.

I sling it around my neck before opening the bedroom door next to me. There I find the most perfect child curled up in bed, her petite hands folded beneath her chubby cheek as she sleeps peacefully.

My chest tightens, disbelief hitting me like always when I think about the fact that I helped create her.

Gently closing the door, I continue down the hall and enter my room to find my other reason for living. The woman I've been in love with since we were teenagers. Julia lies curled up much the same way our daughter is, peacefully sleeping. I come to stand at the end of our bed, admiring the slender curve of her body and smooth, bare leg that pokes out beneath the sheet.

Fisting the blankets, I rip them off of her, revealing the sexy, black silk tank top and panties she wore to bed.

She shoots upright with a gasp, long chestnut hair tangling around her pretty face. She blinks at me, her aquamarine eyes quickly narrowing.

"Jesus, Jaxson. You scared the shit out of me." She drops to her back again, draping an arm over her tired eyes.

Yep. She still hates mornings.

She peeks up at me from beneath her arm, her face pinched in annoyance, but there's no denying the heat in her eyes as they wander over my bare chest.

My cock hardens on the spot.

"Why are you tormenting me this early in the morning?" she asks, her voice mussed with sleep.

Smirking, I get rid of the towel from around my neck then drop to my knees. My hands grip her silk-covered hips as I drag her to the end of the bed. Her legs instinctively open for me, giving me what I seek.

What I fucking own.

I kiss up the inside of her thigh, nipping at her delicate skin, leaving my mark.

Moaning, her hands drive into my hair, fingers gripping and pulling me to the sweet spot between her legs.

Refusing to waste time, I rip the thin silk from her hips and bury my mouth in the sweetest pussy I've ever tasted.

Her flavor, the one I fucking crave, explodes on my tongue, catapulting me into ecstasy.

A harsh gasp parts her lips, her back arching in pleasure. "Jaxson." The breathless sound of my name purging from her delicate throat echoes through the room, fueling my need for more.

I lift my mouth, replacing it with my hand, and give her bare pussy a light slap.

"Oh god!" Her back bows, hips lifting—

begging.

My finger teases her clit, the slick nub hardening further. "Lift your shirt, Julia." The order is rough; need darkening my voice. "Show me your tits."

She does as I say, the black satin clearing her flat stomach and over her head. Her hands caress her skin, giving me a show before she covers herself, fingers pinching the tight little points.

"That's it, baby," I praise. "Play with those pretty nipples for me."

A needy whimper escapes her as she follows the order. "Jaxson, please."

"What do you want, Jules? This?" I give her pussy another slap, watching her soft skin turn pink.

Her scream of pleasure sounds through the room, hips restless—wild. "More," she begs, panting. "Make me come."

Growling, I lay down another smack, the hardest one yet, then cover her with my mouth, my tongue curling around her throbbing clit.

She falls apart beneath me, her cries of pleasure penetrating my mind and heart. Once her tremors subside, I lift her into my arms and carry her into the bathroom.

She wraps her legs around my waist, wet pussy

gliding along my stomach as she kisses up my jaw. A primal need claims me; lust roaring in my veins as I start the shower. I shed my sweats quickly then step inside, pin her against the wall, and drive up into her with one hard thrust.

She cries out, her breath leaving her in a rush. My groan tears apart my chest, head swimming with pleasure.

It's always like this.

No matter how long it's been or how many times I take her, it rocks the very fucking foundation of who I am.

Every—single—time.

Hot water rains down on us, steam billowing and thickening the air, mixing with the passion that's always between us.

"I love you so much," she breathes the words against my lips, her forehead resting on mine.

"I love you too, baby. Now and forever."

My hips surge forward, stealing the air from her lungs once more.

"God." Her head drops back on the wall, pleasure washing over her face as I give her what we both want.

"You love it, Jules, don't you? Love it when my cock feeds this hungry pussy."

"So much," she admits shamelessly. "It's always so good."

"Always, baby. Because it's us."

"Yes!" Her legs grip my hips tighter, arms hugging me closer. "Give it to me. I want it hard."

Her words fuel the beast within me, giving me permission to unleash him. I fuck her right into the wall, my cock relentless with every hard thrust.

"Yes!" Her pussy grips me, sucking me in further.

My hand dips between the smooth crevice of her ass, finger seeking the entrance hidden there. It slips in easily, the water helping with resistance.

"Oh god, I'm going to come again," she cries out the warning.

"Damn right you are and you're going to do it all over my cock."

She careens over the edge for a second time, her fingers biting into my shoulders.

Fire licks down my spine, the sting of her nails taking me along with her. I bury my face into her neck with a groan, giving everything that belongs to her, especially the organ inside my chest.

She rests her cheek next to my temple, lips close to my ear. "Mmm, I love it when we start our mornings like this."

I lift my head, her eyes penetrating me where I stand. They break through every defense I've ever had. "I love every morning that I get to wake up next to you."

The smile she gives me feeds the darkest parts of me, parts that are reserved only for her.

My hand rests against her wet satin cheek before I take her mouth in a slow, deep kiss, a complete contradiction to how I just took her body.

I will never tire of this, never tire of her, and I will cherish it until the day I die.

CHAPTER TWO

Julia

After applying the finishing touches to my hair and make-up, I move into my closet and slip on my white knee-length skirt, baby blue tank top, and white lace flats. A couple squirts of my favorite perfume and I'm ready for my day.

I make my way downstairs into the kitchen, finding the two people I love most in the world at the table. Annabelle sits perched on Jaxson's lap, her small arm wrapped around his neck as she eats her breakfast with him. I bite back a chuckle when I notice her big pink bow is upside down in her curly brown hair.

"Then I told mean ol' Toby to take a hike or I'd give him a what for," she says, shaking her fist as she relays the altercation that took place yesterday on the playground with Toby McDonald. A boy who is never very nice to the other kids.

"Did he listen?" Jaxson asks, a furious bite to his tone.

"No. He laughed at me."

"Laughed at you?" he repeats, outraged.

"Yeah, *laughed at me*. So that did it. I was gonna show him who he was messin' with, but then Beck and Parker showed up and he ran off."

Jaxson grunts. "He wasn't so tough anymore, was he?"

"No, sir. He's such a meanie."

"He sounds like a real asshole."

I gasp, my mouth dropping.

Jaxson's head snaps left, his eyes connecting with mine.

"Uh-oh," Annabelle whispers, her tiny voice laced with amusement.

"Uhh… I meant, what a jerk."

I stalk over to him, ignoring the hum within my body as his eyes sweep from head to toe. Not even an hour ago this man was inside of me, and already, I want more.

"Pay up, now," I demand, holding my hand out.

He drops a kiss on my palm, making Annabelle giggle and me smile.

"Nice try but I don't think so. Five bucks for the swear jar, mister."

"Pay up, Daddy."

Jaxson looks back at Annabelle. "I thought you were on my side."

"Usually I am but Hope, Mia, Ella, and I are saving up for a clubhouse. Between all of our swear jars we almost have enough money."

It takes everything in me not to burst out laughing.

Grunting, Jaxson shifts in his chair and pulls out his wallet. After placing the money in my hand, he lifts Annabelle over his head, making her squeal and laugh, her dress flipping up in the process.

"You want a clubhouse, baby girl. I'll build you one. A far better one than money can buy."

"You mean it, Daddy?"

"Yeah but on one condition."

"What?"

"You must give me a kiss."

Her smile brightens. "Easiest deal I ever made." She squishes his face between her hands and gives him a loud, smacking kiss. "Thanks, Daddy. You're the best."

Jaxson brings her against his chest, holding her close while she gives him a big hug. "Anything for you, Belle. Always."

Love explodes through my chest, dancing to

the tips of my fingers. I'm almost tempted to give him back his money…almost. Instead, I slip it in my skirt pocket.

"You ready to go, sweet girl?" I ask, hating to break up their moment.

"Ready!"

Reaching down, I lift her into my arms. Jaxson's fingers slip into the waistband of my skirt, pulling me in close. A smile steals my lips, knowing exactly what he wants.

Bending down, I lay a long, drawn-out kiss on his mouth like I do every morning before walking out of this house.

"Bye," I whisper, keeping my lips close.

"Be safe."

"Always." Straightening, I turn to leave the room but not before Jaxson's hand lands on my ass, delivering a parting smack.

I swear the man lives to torture me.

"Bye, Daddy. See you after school." Annabelle waves to him over my shoulder.

"Bye, baby girl. Remember, take no shiii… crap from anyone."

"Don't worry, I got this," she assures him.

I shake my head but can't contain another smile.

Once we step out onto the porch, I place

Annabelle to her feet and fix her bow so it's the right way.

She looks up at me sheepishly, her eyes the same ice blue color as Jaxson's. "I knew it was the wrong way but I didn't want to hurt Daddy's feelings. He tries so hard but this is just one thing he can never get right."

I chuckle, warmth filling my heart at the love she has for her father and his pride. "You're right, he does try hard. We don't have to tell him when it's wrong. We'll just fix it ourselves."

"Good idea."

I drop a kiss on her cheek then take her hand and walk to the Denali. The fresh air and warm sun on my skin adds to the already beautiful morning.

Our first stop is the house next door. Parker and Hope wait on the porch with their backpacks on. Grace kisses and hugs them both then Parker takes his sister's hand, walking her down the steps. He boosts her up into the SUV, something he insists on doing because he doesn't need my help getting in.

Like father, like son.

"Hello, darlings," I greet them.

"Hi, Auntie Julia."

Grace waves to me from the front door, getting ready to head out herself for the day. Ever since she donated her kidney to her younger sister, Sawyer won't let her be the one to open the bakery or work long hours. It miffed Grace at first but she understands he's worried and wants her to take it easy. Thankfully, she has her sisters and Mac to help her.

Next, we head to pick up Mia. She too is waiting on the porch, wearing a white sundress and pink cowgirl boots. If hats were allowed at school, I have no doubt she'd be wearing one to complete her outfit.

Faith walks her to the SUV and helps her up into the booster seat since she's the youngest and still requires one.

"Good morning, everyone," Faith greets us with a smile.

"Hey. You headed to the music school?" I ask.

"No, my first appointment isn't until this afternoon. Alissa and I are going out this morning to do some shopping for the baby's room." Her smile brightens, excitement palpable.

"How fun. Text me pictures of your findings."

"I definitely will." After giving Mia a kiss, she wishes us a good day and heads back inside.

Last, but not least, we drive to pick up Beckett. Which, again, is one house over, all of us spread out across eighty acres on the land we subdivided. We are the perfect example that you can be a family without sharing the same blood.

Beckett walks out of the house just as I pull up, looking as handsome as always in his khaki pants and trendy plaid shirt that's been left unbuttoned, revealing a plain white shirt underneath.

That boy is the spitting image of his father.

Kayla comes barreling out of the house with Ella in her arms, yanking Beckett back for a kiss. Clearly, he tried slipping off without one.

The thought has me chuckling.

Both she and Ella wave at me from the door. One more year and that darling little girl will be with us. She's one year younger than Mia and will be in kindergarten next year.

"Hello, handsome," I greet Beckett as he climbs in.

"Hi, Aunt Julia."

"Is everyone ready to go?"

"Ready!" they all shout at the same time.

I do a quick run through of names like I do every morning, more for fun than anything else. "Parker and Hope?"

"Your favorite twins are in the house," Parker

belts out, making everyone laugh.

"Mia?"

"Here."

"Beckett?"

"Check."

I'm about to call the last name but Annabelle speaks first. "Right behind ya, Mama."

Smiling, I slip my sunglasses back on. "All right. Let's go."

The kids talk amongst themselves on the short drive to school, making plans on where to meet at recess. It warms my heart knowing how close they all are, just like us parents.

If someone would have told me ten years ago I would be married to the man I've loved since I was a teenager, have a beautiful daughter with him, and work as a school counselor, I would have never believed them.

But I am.

I'm living the dream. A life I will always be thankful for.

I pull up to Foothills Elementary, parking in my usual spot, then climb out and open the back door. Annabelle gets out first, using my hand as a crutch to jump down.

I kiss each child's cheek, wishing them a good day, and make sure to give Parker two because I know how much he loves it…not!

"Aw, man, come on, Auntie," he complains, wiping his cheek, but there's no hiding his smile.

Unlike Parker, Beckett accepts the affection but is just as uncomfortable with it.

Sheesh, these boys. It's not like I do it in front of the entire school.

Most of them run to play at the park for a few minutes before the bell rings while I take Mia's hand and walk her over to her kindergarten door, which is on the other side of the school.

"I love your boots, are they new?" I ask.

"Yes, ma'am. Kistipher bought them to go with the hat he got me at the market."

"Well that was awfully nice of him."

"Yeah, he loves me."

Her response makes me chuckle.

This sweet little girl is loved by many.

My attention draws to the drop-off zone where I see Connor Daniels climbing out of his mother's car. He moved here only a few months ago. He's a quiet child but very kind.

His mother came to see me when he first transferred here, letting me know he has some social anxiety due to all the moving around they do. She didn't elaborate why they've had to move around so much but I've made sure to do my best to make him feel welcome.

He's in grade two like Annabelle and she has also gone out of her way to include him.

My smile is bright as I greet him. "Good morning, Connor."

"Hi, Mrs. Reid," he mumbles, head down.

"Annabelle is over on the playground if you want to join her."

He nods and heads that way.

The bell rings as I make it to Mia's door so I walk her right inside and into her classroom, waving to her teacher, Leslie Foster.

"Hey, Julia, do you have a quick minute?"

"Sure." Giving Mia a hug good-bye, I hang back and wait for Leslie.

She dodges all the little bodies as they pile into the classroom before stepping out into the hall with me. "I'd like to come by your office at lunch, if that's okay. I'm concerned about one of my students and think things at home need to be looked into."

"Of course. Do you want me to bring Doug in on this meeting?" I ask, talking about the principal.

"Sure, that's fine."

"Okay. We'll meet you in my office at lunch."

"Thanks."

"You bet."

Once she disappears back into the classroom, I start toward the office and see Annabelle walking into her class.

"Have a good day, sweetheart."

"I will, Mama," she calls over her shoulder.

Smiling, I round the corner, running smack into a brick wall. The impact is so hard that I lose my breath for a moment.

Large hands grab my shoulders, making me realize I ran into someone.

"I am so sorry. I didn't…" I trail off as I look up into the face of a man I've never seen before. An older gentleman with salt and pepper hair. He's dressed in an expensive black suit with sunglasses shielding his eyes, looking completely out of place here.

Alarm bells bang around inside of me.

"No problem, dear. It was my fault," he says, flashing me a smile that does nothing to ease my apprehension.

His accent is thick.

Russian? Swedish?

"Can I help you with something?" I ask, wondering why he'd be here.

"No. That's quite all right. I was just dropping off my grandson."

"Grandson?"

"That's right. His babushka and I just got in late last night."

I guess that's why I don't recognize him.

I'm about to ask him who his grandson is but he excuses himself and steps around me, heading out the side entrance. Not the front.

I continue to the main office, my uneasiness lingering.

Janice, the secretary, smiles at my entrance. "Hey, Julia."

"Hey. Did you notice that man out in the hall?" I ask, jerking my thumb over my shoulder.

"What man?"

"He wore a dark suit and sunglasses. Said he was dropping off his grandson…"

"I didn't see him but I was just in the backroom making some photocopies for Mr. Thompson."

I walk around the front desk and look at the security monitors that cover all exits, finding no one in sight.

"Is everything okay?" she asks.

"Yeah, I think so. He just caught me off guard since I've never seen him before."

"I'll keep an eye out. If I see him again, I'll let you know."

"Thanks."

As I head into my office next door, my phone dings with a text. Digging it out of my purse, my heart leaps when I see it's from Jaxson.

> **Jax:** Tonight, we're going to have a repeat of this morning, and I'm going to fuck you so hard you'll be screaming my name.

A ridiculous blush heats my cheeks, my thoughts running wild with all the feelings this man evokes in me.

> **Me:** I hope you make good on this promise, Mr. Reid.
>
> **Jax:** Count on it, baby.
>
> **Me:** Love you.
>
> **Jax:** Not as much as I love you.

He's very wrong about that.

Turning my phone on silent, I slip it into my skirt pocket and open the door to the tall oak cabinet where I hang my purse and store my belongings. I remain standing, my hand over my heart as the Pledge of Allegiance echoes over the intercom.

Afterward, I crack open my windows and take another look around outside, unable to shake my uneasiness from earlier. But again, I see nothing.

Shaking my head, I take a seat at my desk and go through the files I have pulled out for the children I plan to check in on today.

Less than an hour later, there's a slight knock on my open door.

My head snaps up to see Connor Daniels, his face ghost white. "Connor, what is it? What's wrong?"

"Mrs. Reid, I-I think I need help," he says, his voice shaking.

I stand, his fear bringing me to my feet. "Okay. Come in and tell me what's wrong."

Before he can speak, all the lights shut off and so does my computer.

"I think they've found me," he whispers.

Before I can decipher what that means, a scream of terror pierces the air, followed by a gunshot.

Panic pounds in my ears, my knees threatening to give out beneath me.

Grabbing Connor, I yank him into the room then slam my door and lock it. I move to the windows next, closing up every single one.

No alarm goes off, no call comes over the intercom. Nothing but chaos sounds behind my door.

"Connor, come here." Opening up my cabinet, I usher him inside. "I want you to stay in here and don't come out until I tell you to. Do you understand?"

He nods, his brown eyes wide with fear.

"It's going to be okay, I promise. Just don't come out unless I say so. No matter what."

"Okay."

After closing the door, I reach for the phone on my desk but get no dial tone. It's then I realize all the power to the school has been cut.

I dig into my pocket for my cellphone just as another gunshot rings out, this one shooting off the handle on my door.

I jump, a scream ripping from my throat as my door swings open, revealing a man dressed in a black suit and sunglasses, similar to the one I ran into earlier.

He aims his gun right at my chest. "Raise your hands and come out now. Or you die."

I follow the deep, accented order, praying Connor stays where he is. My steps are slow, too slow, so he reaches in and yanks me out the door.

"Faster, bitch!"

Dread seizes my chest when I see there are at least a dozen of them, ushering all the classes into the gym at gunpoint. The children follow in a single line, tears streaking down their pale faces.

My eyes scan the crowd, frantically searching for Annabelle and the others. As we pass the office, I look in and find Janice's head down on the desk, lying in a pool of her own blood.

A strangled noise works its way up my throat, my blood running cold as I comprehend how much trouble we are in.

What started out like every other morning has turned into everyone's worst nightmare, flipping the town of Sunset Bay upside down.

CHAPTER THREE

Jaxson

"I'm tellin' ya, Slade. You need to rethink your retirement," Sarge says, eating his burrito as he follows Kolan through the gym.

"I told you, it's not happening. I'm done fighting."

Sawyer, Cade, and I listen to the two argue while standing at the front counter, going over today's schedule before the gym opens.

"Do you have any idea how much money we could make together?"

"I don't need money. I have more than enough."

Sarge comes to a stop, swallowing his massive bite. "Well excuse me, Mr. Selfish. Do you have any idea how much money *I* could make off your ass? You're a fightin' machine. It's what you're meant to do."

Slade shakes his head, refusing to argue anymore.

"All right, fine," Sarge grumbles. "No fighting. But I still think we should start our own Dark Warrior clothing line. We could sell it right here at the gym. Maybe even get some little tops for the ladies." He delivers the suggestion with a waggle of his eyebrows.

"Yeah and I'll make sure to get one for your woman to sleep in."

The three of us chuckle at the jab but Sarge finds it less than amusing.

I take the opportunity to cut in. "This isn't a fucking mall. The only items we sell here are gloves and supplements. And it's going to stay that way."

"Thank you," Slade says, nodding at me.

"Fine. If you assholes don't wanna make money and support your families, see if I care."

"Hey, who the hell said I don't support my family?" Sawyer bristles, taking offense.

Sarge shrugs. "No one. But let's not forget your wife has a successful bakery."

Sawyer straightens from the counter and points his finger at him. "Let's get one thing straight. I bought my wife that bakery. I also fucked her damn good this morning, gave my kids money to buy themselves a treat at school, and put money in the fucking swear jar."

My brow lifts, realizing we had a similar morning.

"We're like the fucking Brady Bunch at my house," he continues, all fired up. "So take that and shove it up your ass."

"Calm your shit," Cade cuts in. "We all make more than enough to support our families, Sarge included."

"Exactly," I back him up, throwing a look over at Sarge. "You're welcome for that."

"Did I say I was ungrateful? No, I didn't."

"Then what are you saying? Where's all this coming from?"

Sighing, he drops down on the edge of the ring, shoulders slumped. "It's Miranda," he says, talking about his girlfriend who also happens to be Logan's mom. "She wants to move in together."

"What's wrong with that? You guys have been together for what, two years?"

"Two years and four months," he mumbles like a chick. "And hello, that shit costs money."

"Sarge, you make more than enough to rent a place with her," Kolan says. "And she works, too. Between the two of you, everything will be fine."

"Easy for you to say. You don't know what it's

like to sleep on the streets. You wanna know why I eat so many of these?" he asks, holding up his burrito. "Because every morning, when I woke up outside that place to people throwing their garbage at me, I swore if I ever got the opportunity to clean myself up, I'd be the one buying the burrito, not wearing it."

It pisses me off to hear people threw garbage at him but it doesn't surprise me. There are some real assholes out there.

"They also taste really good so that's why I eat them, too," he adds, taking another bite.

"Look. We wouldn't let you end up on the street," I tell him. "You're still going to be able to buy your burritos every morning and live with your girlfriend."

"That's right," Sawyer says, jumping back in. "And you're going to get laid even more. Just think of all the places you'll get to fuck each other. The kitchen table, counter, shower, up against the wall…"

I shoot him a look, letting him know we get the point.

He shrugs. "Just sayin'."

"You're right," Sarge sighs. "We'll be fine, and it's time, I suppose. Can't live here forever."

"You can if you need to," I tell him. "But do

you love her?"

"Of course I do. That's why I'm so damn nervous. I want to take care of her but what if I fuck up?"

"If she loves you then she'll forgive you," Sawyer says. "Grace forgives me all the time for the stupid shit I do."

"And just think of all the dumb shit he does," Cade adds, making us all break into a chuckle.

Several sirens suddenly pierce the air, cutting into the conversation. They sound close. Too close for comfort.

The three of us share a look and step outside to see what's going on. At least a dozen police cruisers speed past the gym. There's so many of them that I swear half of the Charleston department is here, too.

"What the fuck is going on?" Cade mumbles as we watch them disappear around the corner.

It's then my phone vibrates in my pocket. Pulling it out, I see it's Cooper. I hit accept and bring it to my ear. "Coop, what's happening?"

"Get to the kids' school, now!" That's all he says before hanging up on me.

My stomach bottoms out, icy terror flooding my veins.

"What did he say?" Sawyer asks.

My eyes meet theirs as I slip the phone back in my pocket. "It's the school." I barely manage the words through the fear restricting my throat.

We don't waste time climbing into our vehicles and instead go on foot, our shoes pounding the pavement as we run to the school that's only blocks away.

"Did he say what happened?" Cade asks.

I shake my head, unable to speak. Millions of scenarios run through my mind as I try to figure out what it could be.

A fire?

But why all the cops? And I didn't see any fire trucks. My gut tells me it's worse than that. Much worse.

We arrive less than three minutes later. Dozens of cops surround the place, setting up police tape and barricades around the school.

I spot Cooper and Logan in the midst and head their way.

An officer I don't recognize moves to step in front of us, blocking our way. I barrel right through him, shoving him to his ass in the process.

"Cooper!" I call out.

The moment he turns around, my heart stops beating altogether, a fear I've never seen from him prominent in his eyes.

"We have reports that shots have been fired," he says, the words penetrating the blood roaring in my ears. "Gunmen inside. We have no idea how many but we know there are more than one."

My knees buckle at the information, the entire world crumbling beneath my feet as I think about my wife and daughter trapped inside with whatever evil lurks behind those doors.

CHAPTER FOUR

Julia

The air in the gym is stifling, thick with terror of the unknown. I found Annabelle and the rest of the children quickly and rounded them up to keep them close to me.

Annabelle sits on my lap, her tears soaking my shoulder and small body trembling in fear.

A fear I feel all the way to my bones.

Mia is curled up against my side, her tiny fingers clutching my skirt as I hold her close. Beckett sits on my other side with Hope next to him then Parker. Both boys have their arms around her, hugging her as she cries into her knees.

I've never felt more helpless in my life. I've been reassuring them as much as I can but how do you instill safety at a time like this?

At least thirty minutes have gone by but it feels like days and we still have no idea what they want or why they're here. Only a few of the gunmen reside in the gym with us while the others patrol the hallways and cover exits. The man who I ran into earlier this morning, the one I wish I had reported, has been calling the shots.

He barks out orders, speaking in his own language. It looks like they are searching for something, or rather, someone.

I have a feeling I know who that someone is.

My eyes close, remembering Connor's words to me before all hell broke loose. I'm praying he stays where he is and doesn't come out until it's safe to do so.

Hopefully, that's soon. The police are here, we heard the sirens minutes ago, surely they have a plan to get us out of here.

Jax is going to be beside himself when he gets wind of this. The entire town will be, but especially all the people I hold close to my heart. The ones whose children I'll do everything in my power to protect.

Another gunman stalks into the gym, shaking his head at the man in charge.

"It looks like we are going to have to do this the hard way," he says, his voice carrying across the gym.

The room falls quiet except for the children's

sobs.

"I am looking for my grandson, Ivan Mogilevich. Or who you may all know as Connor Daniels."

My stomach tightens as my suspicion is confirmed.

"Who is going to tell me where I can find him?"

Silence remains but the terror is deafening.

Mr. Thompson stands, beads of sweat dotting his forehead. "No one by either of those names go to this school."

His lie prompts a malicious smirk on the other man's face, putting his feet in motion. He stops just in front of Mr. Thompson, crowding his personal space. "You are the principal, yes?"

"That's correct. I know all the children in this school and not one of them go here by that name."

The man reaches inside his jacket and pulls out his gun, holding it to Mr. Thompson's forehead.

Oh God.

"Do you want to answer that question again?"

My heart lodges in my throat, horror washing over me. "Turn away," I whisper to the kids, my blurry eyes frozen on the men before me. "Do it now. Close your eyes."

Mr. Thompson swallows hard, his entire body trembling, but he holds his ground. "I could but my answer will be the same. There are no—"

The gun goes off, echoing through the gym. Screams explode through the air and mingle with my own.

I cover the children, sobs ripping apart my chest as I watch Doug hit the floor, his blood pooling beneath his lifeless body.

"Who's next?" the man bellows. He trains his gun around the room, landing on Mrs. Foster, Mia's kindergarten teacher. "You. Tell me where my grandson is or you die, too."

Crying, Leslie shakes her head from where she sits with her class in the corner of the gym. "I don't know him. He's not one of my students."

"Well, I guess that's too bad for you."

"No, stop! Please," I plead out loud. "She's telling the truth."

The man turns to me, recognition dawning in his eyes. "Ah, you, from this morning."

"She doesn't know who he is but I do. You're right, he is a student at this school, but he didn't show up today. I saw the list of absences this morning."

He stares back at me, searching for the truth.

I hold his gaze, willing for him to believe it, because right now it's our only hope.

"If what you say is true then it seems we have a very big problem here."

The cold, calculating look in his eyes sends my stomach plummeting. Any hope I just had diminishes and I fear for what's to come.

CHAPTER FIVE

I pace the cement like a caged animal, everything inside of me falling apart. A crowd has gathered outside the school and it continues to grow with each minute that passes. Word of mouth has always traveled fast in this town.

The property is surrounded not only by squad cars of the local police but fire trucks and ambulances, waiting and ready if necessary. Cooper barks out commands, trying to keep order while we wait for more information to come in.

Logan comes up to me, his hand going to my shoulder. "It's okay, man. We'll get them out of there."

It's not okay. There's nothing *okay* about any of this.

"What the fuck are we waiting for?" Sawyer asks. "We should be in there, not out here."

"We need to know what we're dealing with,"

Logan says, being the voice of reason. "We can't just go in guns blazing."

"Why not? It's worked for us every other time."

I'm with Sawyer on this one. I become more restless with each second that passes. Ready for battle, to shed the blood of the bastards who dare to threaten the lives of innocent children and the people I love most.

My attention shifts to Cade, waiting for him to weigh in but he remains silent, pacing as restlessly as me. He's been quiet the entire time but the fear and rage in his eyes mirrors the one hammering through my veins.

"Sawyer!" Grace's frantic voice breaks through the chaos as she runs from across the street in her bakery dress, her panic-stricken face ashen with fear.

An officer intercepts her, grabbing her shoulders to hold her back.

It sends Sawyer in motion. "Get your fucking hands off my wife." He surges forward, grabbing the officer by the back of his shirt and throwing him against one of the police cruisers.

"Evans, back off." Cooper jumps between them. "He's just doing his job. He doesn't know who she is."

"I don't give a shit. No one touches her. *Ever.*"

Cooper orders for another officer to let Grace through.

She rushes over to Sawyer, tears staining her cheeks. "Tell me it's not true. Tell me there are not gunmen in our children's school."

He remains silent; unable to speak the words she longs to hear, what we all wish wasn't true. Her forehead falls to his chest, overcome with grief.

Faith and Alissa show up next, making a beeline for Cade. The officer is smart enough this time to lift the tape and let them through.

"Cade, what's happening?" Faith asks, emotion thick in her voice. "Someone said there's been a shooting."

He opens his mouth to speak but nothing comes out. Clearing his throat, he tries again. "I'm going to get her, Red. I swear, I'll get her out of there."

"Oh God!" A sob tumbles from Faith.

He pulls her in close, whispering promises into her ear.

I shake my head, feeling so fucking helpless. "What's the hold up, Coop? What's taking so long?"

"The phone line has been cut. We can't get through to anyone inside. SWAT's on its way and so is their negotiator. We—"

A gunshot explodes from the school, the distant sound slamming into me like a freight train.

Grace drops to her knees on a scream; gut-wrenching sobs ripping from her chest. Sawyer covers her, his arms banding tight around her body.

"You have to get them, Sawyer. You have to get our babies out of there," she cries.

All of us share a look, making a silent agreement.

No more waiting.

"Sheriff McKay?"

We turn to find a man in a suit pushing past the police tape.

Cooper eyes him up. "Yeah?"

He flashes his badge. "Special Agent Dobson. We're here to take over."

"Take over?"

"That's right. Since your son is in that school you are being removed from this case."

His arrogance sends Cooper forward. "I don't think so, motherfucker."

Logan intercepts him, holding him back.

"I don't take orders from you or anyone else.

This is my fucking town!"

"He's right," Ryder says, shouldering through the crowd with Nick following close behind him. "You aren't the one who has been appointed in charge of this case, Dobson. We are, and we say Sheriff McKay stays."

Dobson's jaw flexes, teeth grinding. "The chief said—"

"It doesn't matter," Nick cuts him off. "The sheriff stays. He and his men know this town and its people better than anyone."

"Cooper!" The call comes from Kayla as she pushes through the throng of people and ducks under the tape, launching herself into Cooper's waiting arms. "Ella is with my mom. I left as soon as you called."

My phone vibrates in my pocket, dragging my attention away. Pulling it out, my heart stops when I see whom it's from.

"It's Julia," I announce.

Everyone surrounds me as I swipe the screen to read the text.

Jules: *All of the children are safe and with me.*

"Thank God," Faith cries, burying her face into Cade's chest.

Before I have a chance to reply, she sends

another one.

> They're holding us in the gym. All of them have accents. I think they're Russian but can't be certain.
>
> **Me:** How many?
>
> **Jules:** If I counted correctly, 14.

"Fourteen? Who the hell are these assholes?" Sawyer asks, voicing my thoughts.

> **Jules:** They need to hurry, Jax. Janice and Mr. Thompson are dead. They shot him in front of the children minutes ago. They're growing impatient.

Her fear bleeds through her words, making me feel even more fucking helpless.

> **Me:** Hang tight, baby. We're coming for you. Have they said what they want?

We stand by, waiting for her response but it never comes. I debate on texting again but I don't want to draw attention to her.

Looking up, I make eye contact with Coop, Cade, and Sawyer. "Let's go. We'll load up at my house."

I push forward, resolution burning in my veins.

"Just wait a goddamn minute." Dobson grips my shoulder, halting my pursuit.

Spinning around, I grab the bastard by the throat and drop him to the pavement. "You ever put your hands on me again I will rip out your fucking spine."

"You have no command here," he wheezes out.

My fingers squeeze his throat, an inch away from shattering his windpipe as I lean in closer. "My wife and daughter are in that school and no one will fight harder for their lives than me. So take your pissing match somewhere else or I will fucking end you in my path of destruction."

"Easy now," Nick says calmly, pulling me back. "Come on, you can suit up with us. We'll go in together."

"That's against orders, Stone," Dobson snaps. "This is SWAT's job and no one else's."

"SWAT isn't here and we aren't waiting any longer," Ryder says. "We're going in now."

I follow behind them, thankful that I don't have to waste time going home. Nick motions for Knight to follow while the others kiss their wives, reassuring them everything will be okay.

I wish I could do the same for Julia, to tell her everything will be okay. I have no doubt she's terrified out of her fucking mind right now but being brave enough for all the children inside.

"Cade!" Christopher shows up, hurdling over the police tape. "Are we going in?" he asks, ready for battle like the rest of us.

"Yeah, follow us."

Nick leads us to a black, tinted-out SUV that's hidden behind news vehicles. Ryder opens the hatch, unveiling a selection of weapons. He starts tossing us vests, ear sets, and lets us have our choice of gun.

Meanwhile, Nick flips open a laptop, bringing up an image of a floor plan. "This is the most updated version of the school I could find. There are seven entrances, all have surveillance to them but we've been told they've been disabled," he says, looking at Coop.

Cooper nods. "All the power has been cut but I'm assuming the backup generators are running. We've been able to detect that all entrances are being guarded from the inside."

"What if we go in from the roof?" I suggest. "We can go through the air ducts and split off in different directions."

"Half of us take out the entrances and the rest have eyes in the gym," Cade says.

"I'm taking the gym," I cut back in, both

Sawyer and Cade making the same statement.

Ryder nods. "All right. But we take no one out unless we're forced to, got it?"

We remain silent, refusing to make that promise.

"I'm serious. I know you guys are pissed off, we all are. But we do this by the book."

"I tell you what, Jameson," I start, trying to rein in my temper. "You go ahead and do it by the book. You're an officer of the law. I'm not. I was trained to kill for the sake of this country. I also took that vow when it comes to my family. So I will do whatever it takes to free the people inside."

"That's what we all plan to do, Reid." Nick steps in, defending him. "This isn't a fucking war zone. Rules need to be followed."

"Those rules were thrown out the moment those bastards walked into that school and threatened the lives of innocent people, especially our kids," I bellow. "They deserve no fucking mercy."

"Our first priority is the safety of everyone inside, even before making the bad guys pay."

"What if this were Katelyn?" I ask him. "What if your son was sitting in that school with guns pointed at him? Would you follow your goddamn rules then?"

"We care about your kids, too," he says. "We're all family here, which is why Ryder and I are going against orders and letting you guys be a part of this."

"And we appreciate that," Cooper adds, his hand going to my shoulder. "We all want the same thing here. The safety of everyone inside comes first."

Nick holds my stare. "We're with you on this, Reid. I plan to do everything in my power to save your family along with everyone else in that school."

Pushing my anger aside, I nod, knowing he doesn't deserve it. Without them, I wouldn't be going into that school as quick as I am.

"Jameson," an agent calls out, pushing his way toward us. "I have someone here with information for you." He thrusts a petite blonde woman in front of him. Tears stream down her face, her eyes wide with fear. "This is Monica Daniels."

"Ms. Daniels," Ryder greets her, shaking her hand.

"I know who's inside and what they want," she says, her voice thick with emotion.

"Who?"

"His name is Dimitri Mogilevich, he's from Moscow and head of the mafia there."

I tense, my gut clenching at the information.

"Tell me, Ms. Daniels, what would bring someone like him to this small town?"

"He wants my son," she chokes out. "We've been running from him for almost six years."

"Why?"

"Because I killed his son to escape my prison of a marriage," she tells us. "Dimitri is my son's grandfather and he wants him back in Moscow with him." Her composure breaks, a sob tumbling past. "I didn't mean for this to happen. I was so sure he'd never find us here. I don't even live in Sunset Bay. I live in Oakbrook and drive out of my way every morning."

Ryder places his hand on her shoulder. "It's all right. We're going to get your son out of there. I want you to stay with Special Agent Cranston. He's going to take you somewhere safe and we'll bring your son to you when we have him."

She shakes your head. "You don't understand. He'll stop at nothing to get Connor. He's dangerous."

"So am I," I tell her, fingers gripping the rifle I hold. "And I'll stop at nothing to get my family back."

Slipping my earpiece in, I push forward with only one thought in mind...

Vengeance.

CHAPTER SIX

Julia

It has become so hot in the gym that the children grow thirsty, sweat soaking through their clothes. The girls are in sundresses but I had Beckett and Parker remove their button-up shirts, leaving them in their undershirts.

"I want my daddy," Hope cries, her muffled sobs breaking my heart.

"Me, too," Mia says, her small face tucked against my side where it's been the whole time.

I reach over Beckett for Hope's hand while the boys continue to console her. "I know you guys are scared," I whisper. "But we're going to get through this. I promise. I sent Uncle Jax a text. He says they're coming for us. We just have to be strong until they can get in here."

I sent the text almost ten minutes ago. I didn't communicate for long, fearing I'd get caught, but I had to let them know we were okay.

"My dad's gonna throw all their asses in jail," Beckett says, his small voice tight with anger.

I don't bother scolding him for his language because he has every right to feel angry right now.

"My dad will shoot them," Parker says.

"Mine, too." Annabelle sniffles, lifting her head from my shoulder. "And I don't even feel bad about that."

My eyes close, fear plaguing me at the thought of what all the guys will do when they get in here. For the sake of the children, I pray for as minimal violence as possible. They've seen enough to last them a lifetime.

"My daddy is probably so sad," Mia cries, wiping her wet cheeks. "He always worries about somethin' bad happenin' to us."

That's every parent's worst fear and all of Sunset Bay is living that nightmare right now. This one horrific moment will irrevocably change us all, especially the children.

My attention draws to the two men in the center of the gym, where they speak in hushed tones. The man in charge becomes more agitated by the second. His eyes shift to me, making my heart jump in my chest as he heads over to us.

Annabelle gasps, hiding her face in my shoulder. I hold her close, keeping my eyes on the man before me.

"You," he says, pointing at me. "Come."

"No!" Annabelle cries, hugging my neck tighter.

"Why?"

"You do not ask questions. Come, now!"

I press a kiss to Annabelle's cheek. "It'll be okay, baby. Stay here with the others. I'll be right back."

"No, Mama. Please don't go."

Her heartfelt plea has me choking back a sob. "Annabelle, I need you to be strong right now."

The man becomes angry, sighing in frustration. "Belkov, remove the child from her."

"No!" I snap. "If you put your hands on my daughter I will not help you."

The man's eyes narrow, his gun swinging over to Mia. "You have seconds to stand or the first child of the day dies."

Mia cowers, breaking into hysterics.

Defeat settles over me as I pry Annabelle's grip from around my neck and sit her next to Beckett. I move Mia next to them, making sure they're all close. "Take care of each other. I'll be back soon."

The reassurance barely leaves my mouth when I'm yanked to my feet by my hair. "Time's up."

"Mama!" Annabelle wails, her desperate scream shattering my soul.

Both Parker and Beckett jump to their feet, fists clenched at their sides.

"Let her go!" Parker orders.

"Sit down, boys!" Guilt strikes me for yelling at them but my fear for their lives runs deeper.

"Listen to her. Now is not the time to be brave. I'd hate to have to shoot you both."

A crying Hope grabs their arms and drags them back down next to her. It's the last thing I see before I'm shoved forward, the cold barrel of a gun pressed against the back of my head.

"Mama!"

Looking over my shoulder, I see Beckett holding Annabelle back. Her pleading sobs trigger one of my own.

"Why are you doing this?" I cry, frustrated by their senseless act of cruelty.

"Haven't I made myself clear? I want my grandson back, and I am not leaving this country without him."

"You won't ever make it out of here," I whisper.

"Oh, my dear. That's where you're very wrong. Not only will I have my grandson back but I will also make his mother pay for all the pain she has caused my family."

My eyes close, wishing I had checked into Connor's background more. Maybe if I had this could have all been prevented.

"The police are outside. We all heard them," I say, unable to keep the bite out of my tone.

"Yes, they are, and there is a probability they will even take me to jail for a short time."

"Try a lifetime," I mumble.

If my husband doesn't kill you first.

Grabbing a fistful of my hair, he jerks my head back. "Watch your mouth or I will cut your tongue out and let you bleed to death in front of your daughter."

I'm thrusted into my office, hard enough that I land on top of my desk face first. Pain explodes through my head, the metallic taste of blood filling my mouth.

Before I have time to recover, he grabs me by the back of my neck and shoves me around my desk. My eyes land on the cabinet Connor hides in, willing for him to stay where he is.

"Show me the list of absences," he orders. "I also want my grandson's file with his home address."

"It's not in here," I murmur, blood trickling from my mouth.

His fingers wrap around my neck, squeezing my throat. "Bullshit. This is your office and you said you saw the list of absences. Now stop fucking with me or I will put a bullet in your head then do the same to your daughter."

I'm about to tell him the information is on the powerless computer when Connor pushes out of the cabinet.

"Don't hurt her!"

The man stills, his body tense with surprise. "Ivan?" he asks, a sense of awe in his voice.

"Please," Connor pleads, tears streaking down his pale face. "Don't hurt her. I'll do whatever you want."

The man releases me unconsciously, taking the smallest step forward. "Bhyk," he breathes, his accent thick with emotion. "I can't believe it's really you." He reaches for Connor. "Come. It's time to go home."

Desperation fuels me, putting me in motion. "No!" I push myself between them, taking Connor's hand. "Run, Connor!"

We don't even reach the door before a shot fires off. Pain explodes through my side, seizing all the air in my lungs. Turning, I stare into the face of a cold-blooded killer as he shoots again, spraying another bullet into my abdomen.

The impact throws me back, fire tearing through my entire body, but the pain is nothing to the terror that rips through my heart. A cold realization hitting me that I won't make it out of this alive.

CHAPTER SEVEN

Jaxson

The breadth of my shoulders fill the confined space, my breathing even as I look through small slats of the vent I hide behind. My eyes scan the vacant courtyard that's just outside the gym, a sense of calmness resting over me despite the fear and rage I harbor deep inside.

I sense Sawyer and Cade in their positions, feeling their presence even if I can't see them. It's a flash of déjà vu, bringing me back to a time when we always knew the other was there, watching our back. Only this time there is so much more at stake.

"Entrance two has been silenced and stripped of weapons." Christopher's voice fills the earbuds. "There were two of them."

"Alive?" Ryder asks quietly.

"For now, but we'll see if that lasts."

Ryder grunts. "Keep it that way. Stay where

you are. I want you covering that exit."

"Copy. I'm in the northeast hall and all is clear."

Knight checks in next. "Entrance three has been taken care of."

"I just got word that SWAT showed up," Nick announces, his voice barely above a whisper.

About fucking time.

"They're covering the helicopter and perimeter, waiting for our signal."

We found the helicopter when we made it on the roof, something that was hidden from down below due to the structure of the building. The two men that waited next to it were dismantled of their communication devices and cuffed.

"Entrance one and four are taken care of," Ryder says, sounding out of breath.

"I have five," Cooper says. "There were two here as well."

"I have six and seven," Nick says. "Reid, you guys should be safe to get into position."

The three of us push out of the vents that circle the courtyard and slide out from our spots. We curl behind the walls on either side of the gym doors. Cooper joins us, moving up behind me.

Holding my gun up, I peek in and spot two

men on the right. Their weapons are trained as they walk a straight line back and forth between the children. Seeing the fear on the children's pale faces, fuels the deep-seated anger inside of me.

"I have two in sight," I relay, looking for Julia and the kids.

"We have three in ours," Cade says.

"Half of SWAT is waiting on the east doors that lead inside the gym," Nick says. "I'm going to give them the signal. Once they enter, move in and make sure they're covered."

"Copy," Cooper responds.

Sawyer makes eye contact with me from across the way. "Do you see them?"

I shake my head and try my damnedest not to think too much about that, knowing I need to keep my head straight.

Within seconds, SWAT busts in through the emergency exit of the gym, sending us forward. Screams erupt through the air as everyone is ordered to drop their weapons.

One of the men close to me lifts his gun, pointing it at the swarm of cops. I don't give him a chance to fire, the butt of my rifle slamming into his temple. The rest of them are thrown facedown and cuffed.

"Daddy!" The sound of Annabelle's terrified

voice stops me in my tracks, my eyes searching amongst the chaos.

"There!" Cooper points across the gym where all the kids are standing together, holding hands.

We push forward, dodging all the small bodies in our path. I catch a crying Annabelle, scooping her small body into my arms and bringing her in close.

"It's okay, baby," I soothe, burying my nose into her soft brown hair. "Everything is okay now."

"You need to get Mama," she cries.

My eyes wander, looking around for her. "Where is she?"

"They took her," Beckett says.

Every muscle in my body tightens, panic threatening to choke me.

"Who did?" Cooper asks before I can.

"One of the men," Parker tells us. "They dragged her out by her hair."

Ice forms in my veins, my mind reeling as I realize we must have missed one.

"He was hurting her, Daddy," Annabelle sobs. "You have to hurry."

Without a second thought, I thrust Annabelle into Christopher's arms, hating to have to let her go. "Take her outside with the others. I'll be there soon!" I push my way back through the crowded gym, raising my mic to my mouth. "Stone, have you seen Julia?"

"Isn't she with the kids?"

"No. We're missing one of the bastards. Someone has her."

"Jaxson, wait up!" Cooper yells, catching up to me in the hall.

My quick feet never falter. "You should be with Beckett."

"Cade has him. He and Sawyer are coming back once they get the kids outside to the girls."

We come up to hallways on either side of us, and I catch the gun in my peripheral vision before seeing the person behind it. My instincts are quicker than his. Knocking his hand away, I disarm him and take him down, shoving my rifle against his throat. "Where is my wife, you son of a bitch?"

"Go to hell!"

I apply pressure, cutting off his air supply. "You have seconds to tell me where she is or I will cut out your fucking heart and feed it to you."

Nick and Ryder come charging in the front doors the same time we hear a scream.

"No! Run, Connor!"

My head snaps left, the sound of Julia's voice

throwing me into motion. Pushing to my feet, I leave the guy with Ryder and head in the direction of her office, passing both Cooper and Nick. Our boots pummel the tile floor, guns drawn. Halfway there a shot fires off, followed by a second one.

Dread curls its lethal fingers around my heart when I see Julia stumble out the door, her blood-soaked hands covering her stomach.

I have no time to comprehend anything, not even the shouted orders behind me as I lunge for her. My feet leave the floor, gun aiming into the open room. There I come face-to-face with the enemy, his pistol trained on my wife.

I fire off several shots, driving a bullet into the center of his forehead. My arms come around Julia as I take her to the ground with me, shouldering the brunt of our fall.

While the others rush inside the room, I sit up and cradle the top half of her body. "Julia, baby, can you hear me?" I look down at my hands, finding them coated in blood.

"Jax?" Blood spews from her mouth as she tries to speak.

"Shh, don't talk." I cover her gaping stomach, trying to stanch the blood but there's too much. "Get paramedics in here now!" The order barely makes its way past the restriction in my throat, my eyes burning, blurring the woman I hold.

Cooper drops down next to me, trying to help me stop the bleeding.

There's so much fucking blood.

Her breathing is labored; face pale as she peers up at me. "I'm so scared," she cries.

"Don't be scared, baby. I'm here." I kiss her cold, wet cheeks, trying to calm her but everything inside of me is falling apart for a second time today. "It's going to be okay. *You're* going to be okay."

The reassurance is more for myself than her and for the first time in my life, I could very well be lying to her. Every second that passes, more of her blood spills, and I feel her slipping further away from me, taking my mangled heart with her.

CHAPTER EIGHT

Jaxson

Covered in my wife's blood, I sit in the emergency room; my eyes trained ahead—heart cold.

Body numb.

Annabelle is curled against my chest, my arms wrapped securely around her as she sleeps, the day's trauma leaving her depleted.

I drop a kiss on the top of her head, lingering as I breathe in her scent. The same shampoo her mother uses.

Our lives have been changed forever, even more so if my wife doesn't come out of surgery with a beating heart.

The thought has agony ripping through my wounded chest.

Just this morning I touched her, kissed her, loved her the way I promised to do, and to know there is a possibility I will never get to do those things again leaves me feeling dead inside.

I can't live without her. I need her, Annabelle needs her. Without Julia, our family will never be whole.

"What can I do?" Anna asks, her throat raw with grief as she rests her head against my shoulder where she sits next to me.

She and Logan have been here with me since the beginning, answering the phone as everyone else continues to call, anxiously waiting on news like we are.

"Nothing," I croak.

There's nothing anyone can do to make this right. Not unless they can change time and take me back to this morning.

If only I had made it to her a minute sooner, hell, even seconds earlier, I could have prevented that shot. Just like years ago, I was minutes too late for the girl who sits next to me.

The guilt will weigh on me for the rest of my life and so will this ever present rage.

That bastard I took out deserved a hell of a lot more than a bullet between his eyes. I'm not finished. Everyone who had a hand in this will fucking pay.

Revenge will be had and justice will be served by my hands. They will know the same fear and pain they inflicted upon my family.

"Mr. Reid?"

My head snaps up, breath locking in my chest at the sight of the doctor walking in. Beads of sweat dot his forehead beneath his blue cap, his expression somber.

I climb to my feet, unable to say anything, fear paralyzing me. My heart pounds, hammering in my ears as I wait for the verdict that could very well ruin my existence.

"Your wife is going to be okay."

Anna wraps her arms around me, crying in relief, but I remain still, my mind trying to process what he just said.

"It was touch and go for a while. Julia lost a lot of blood and was given several transfusions. We were able to extract the bullets, including the one that was lodged into her intestines. It will take some time but other than a lot of rest and care over the next few weeks, I expect a full recovery."

It isn't until he finishes that I'm able to take in my first full breath. I bury my face in Annabelle's hair, hugging her tight. "We're going to be okay, baby."

She doesn't stir, her body still heavy with sleep, but there's no denying the feel of her tiny heartbeat tapping against my battered one.

My attention reverts back to the doctor. "I want to see her. I want to be with my wife."

He nods. "That can be arranged. She's in recovery now but I will have a nurse come get you soon."

Shifting Annabelle to one arm, I extend my hand to him. "Thank you, for everything."

"You're very welcome. Nurse Betty will be in soon to get you."

Once he leaves the room, Anna hugs me tighter, her arms wrapped around both Annabelle and me. "I knew she would pull through," she cries.

I'm glad one of us did because I wasn't as certain.

"Why don't we take Annabelle home with us?" Logan suggests.

"No."

Anna steps back and tries to reason with me. "Let us take her, Jax. It will give you time with Julia. We can bring her back in the morning."

I shake my head, panic thrumming through my veins at the thought of letting her go.

"I'd never let anything happen to her," Logan adds. "You know that. I'd die for her."

"I know, and I appreciate it, but she stays with Julia and me." The firmness in my tone has them backing off respectfully.

Anna stretches up, kissing my cheek. "We'll come back first thing in the morning and bring you some stuff from home."

"I'd appreciate that. Would you mind calling everyone and letting them know she's going to be okay?"

"Of course. I was already planning on it."

"Thanks."

"Mr. Reid?" the nurse calls as she enters the room. "I can take you to your wife now."

I nod over at Logan and Anna, bidding them good-bye. "I'll see you guys tomorrow. Thanks for everything." My strides are quick as I follow the nurse out, urgency fueling every step.

"I had another bed brought in for your daughter," she says quietly.

"Thank you."

"You're welcome," she whispers, emotion building in her voice. "I'm just so sorry about everything that happened in that school. My heart breaks thinking how scared those poor children must have been."

What happened today affected everyone in this town, a reminder of the monsters that walk among us, waiting to inflict terror.

Monsters I will always be there to take out.

We reach an open door to one of the rooms and it brings me to a cold, hard stop, because there lies my wife with tubes streaming from every angle.

"You can put your daughter here," the nurse whispers, pointing to the bed next to Julia's.

Swallowing thickly, I get my feet moving again and lay Annabelle down.

"I'll be right outside if you need anything," the nurse says, touching my shoulder. "Otherwise, I'll be back in a little while to check on Julia."

I nod, unable to speak past the knot in my throat. Once she disappears, I put one foot in front of the other, my feet mechanical as I take the chair next to Julia's bed.

Grasping her cold, fragile hand, I bring it to my mouth for a kiss but the grief I've been holding in all day rips apart my chest. My head drops down next to her, overcome with despair as the day's events finally catch up to me. I think about how close I came to losing her when I promised long ago I'd never let anyone hurt her again.

It's minutes later when the sound of a whimper penetrates my grief. Lifting my head, I see Annabelle, tossing and turning, a terrified sob purging from her as she sleeps.

I pull myself together and climb into the small bed with her, my large body wrapping around her tiny one. She instantly settles down, burying her face into my chest.

Reaching over her curled body, I grab Julia's hand. For the rest of the night, I remain that way. My tears soak my daughter's hair as I hold my family close, vowing once again to never let anyone take them from me.

CHAPTER NINE

Sawyer

The Evans residence

Blanketed in the dark, I stare up at my bedroom ceiling, emotion battling inside of me. My daughter lies curled up next to me, her fingers gripping my shirt while my son sleeps on the other side of her, wrapped in his mother's arms.

My family is home and safe yet I feel no peace. Relief, yes, but even that is overshadowed by hate, fury, and vengeance.

For years I was groomed to kill and taught how to face the most horrific of circumstances but nothing could have prepared me for what I went through today.

A sniffle breaks into my bleak thoughts. Turning my head, I find Grace awake, crying again as she holds our son. She's been doing this for hours. Dozing off and on, only to wake up grief-stricken.

It makes me feel completely fucking helpless because there aren't any words that will bring her the peace she deserves, just like there is nothing to bring it to me.

I reach over the children and grab her hand. Her fingers squeeze mine while her eyes remain on Parker.

"When I heard that gunshot today," she starts quietly, "I felt that same terror and devastation the day I lost my mama." Her breath hitches as she tries to speak. "And all I could think was, surely God wouldn't do this to me twice. That my babies wouldn't be ripped away from me in the most cruel way."

The sob that flees her has me pushing from my spot in bed and coming over to her side. She turns into me, burying her face against my chest.

"You guys are all I have, Sawyer," she cries. "You're the only ones that make my life worth living. I'd never survive losing y'all."

My jaw flexes, hating the fear and sorrow in her voice. "I swear to you, Grace, I'll never let anyone hurt our family. No one will ever take this from us." The rage that burns within my blood at the thought fucking terrifies me.

Her hand moves to the side of my face, slender fingers fanning my jaw. "I know, and it's only one of the many things that I love about you."

I drop a kiss on her lips, the taste of her tears fueling the ache in my chest. She snuggles in closer to me and it isn't long before her breathing evens out and she falls back asleep.

It's hours later when sleep finally claims me and I'm able to drift off, only to wake up to a blood-curdling scream.

"Daddy!"

In the dark I see Hope sitting upright, screaming at the top of her lungs.

I jump over Grace and Parker to reach her. "Shh, Shortcake. I'm right here."

She crawls onto my lap, her tiny arms squeezing my neck. "Don't leave me," she cries. "Don't ever leave me again."

I bury my face in her hair, a fierce ache burning the back of my throat. "Never, Shortcake. I'll never let you go."

It's a promise I intend to keep until the day my heart fucking stops beating.

CHAPTER TEN

Faith

The Walker residence

Today, evil lurked in this town. It terrorized and threatened but it did not conquer.

Only one other time in my life did I feel the terror and hopelessness that I did while standing outside of that school, and it was the week I spent in Iraq, where my freedom and body were stolen from me. Even back then, evil did not prevail. But knowing this doesn't make it any easier to deal with the horror we all went through today.

Now we sit, waiting with bated breaths, praying for the survival of a family member, one of my best friends. A woman who cared for all of our children when we couldn't be there.

The thought of Julia not pulling through is too devastating to comprehend and it has me crying harder.

"Can I get you more tea?" Alissa asks, curling

an arm around my shoulders.

I shake my head, unable to speak past my flowing tears.

Christopher walks into the kitchen with the phone in his hand, his expression grim. "That was Anna."

My heart lodges in my throat, fear gripping me to hear his answer.

"Julia's going to be okay."

"Oh thank God." The breath I expel explodes on a sob, my knees close to giving out on me.

Christopher gathers me in his arms, offering me the comfort I so desperately need. "Everything is going to be okay, Faith. Everyone is safe."

I nod. "What's happening with Annabelle?"

"She's with Jaxson. Anna said he wouldn't let her go home with them."

I'm not surprised, and I can't say I blame him.

Stepping back, I pull myself together, wiping the remainder of my tears. "I'm going to go let Cade know."

"Alissa and I are going to sleep here tonight," he says. "We'll stay in my old room. If you need anything come get me."

Warmth invades my heart at his kindness. Reaching up, I frame his face between my hands, loving the man he has become. "Thank you for being here."

"This is my family, Faith. I'll always be here."

The softest smile touches my lips before I kiss his cheek then head upstairs to see Cade. A tightness forms in my belly, fearing what kind of shape I will find my husband in.

He's been distant and quiet since returning home. There's a rage in his eyes that I haven't witnessed in years but amongst that fury also lies fear—one he battles every day due to the loss of his sister—the fear of losing the ones he loves.

Walking into our bedroom, I find him lying on the bed with an arm behind his head, his gaze trained on the ceiling. Mia is tucked into his side where he holds her close. Ruthie lies sleeping on the other side of Mia, her arm draped across her sister and Cade's stomach.

The sight brings a small measure of warmth to my heavy heart, that's until Cade's eyes shift from the ceiling and anchor on me. The pain buried in them strikes me all the way to my soul.

My steps are quiet as I start forward. "Anna called," I whisper, "Julia is going to be okay."

His chest deflates as he lets out a painful breath. "Thank christ for one thing going right."

Sitting next to him, my hand moves to his jaw, thumb sweeping over his firm lips. The blankness reflecting back at me leaves me feeling cold and helpless.

"Talk to me."

"About what?"

"About how you're feeling."

His jaw flexes, teeth grinding. "I'm mad, Red. Really fucking mad."

"I can understand that. I'm pretty angry too but I'm also thankful for everyone's safety, especially our children."

"Yeah, until next time."

"Hopefully there will never be one."

"Come on, Red. It's a vicious cycle. This world is fucking heinous. Look at everything we've been through, it never stops."

"Exactly, look at everything we've been through, Cade, and yet here we are, hearts still beating," I whisper, my hand moving to his chest. "Loving each other and raising a family."

He shakes his head, anger tightening his expression. "What if the next time we don't come out on top? What if, after you've done everything in your power to protect your family and keep them safe, it's still not enough? I can't go through that again, Red. Not a second time." His voice breaks, eyes lifting back to the ceiling as he tries to conceal his grief.

Tears cloud my eyes, my heart aching to heal this pain he will always harbor. "At the end of the day all we can do is love one another and live our lives to the fullest. I have to believe that God brought us here for a reason. I have to hold onto that faith, we both do, because without faith there's no hope." My breath hitches as sobs build in my chest.

His eyes shift back to mine, the unshed tears ripping through my wounded heart. He lifts his hand to my cheek, his hard expression softening. "I have all the faith I need right here."

Smiling, I lean into his touch, craving it like I do every day. His hand hooks behind my neck, bringing my lips upon his. He kisses away my tears while I try to inhale all of his fears.

Eventually, I stretch out next to him, barely fitting on what's left of the mattress. His arm bands around my back, tucking me in close to him as my head rests on his chest.

"We got this, Cade," I whisper, slipping my hand under his shirt to feel his warm skin. "We can get through this like we have everything else."

He drops a kiss on the top of my head. "Yeah, Red. We can."

He says that but I know this is something we will always battle, his fear of losing us runs so strong. But every day I will be here, giving him the unwavering love and faith to see him through.

CHAPTER ELEVEN

Cooper

The McKay residence

The night is hot and air stifling as I sit on my front porch, staring out into the quiet dark. I tilt the bottle to my lips for another sip. The amber liquid burns my throat, spreading across my aching chest. I welcome the inferno, trying to mask the guilt that will no doubt plague me for the rest of my life.

I made a vow, a pledge to this town to protect it, and today, I failed.

"Coop?" Kayla's sleepy voice penetrates my misery. The screen door creaks as she steps outside. "What are you doing out here? It's three in the morning."

My eyes remain ahead as I open my mouth to answer, but find I can't speak past the restriction in my throat.

When I don't answer, she steps down and

K.C. LYNN

comes to kneel in front of me. Blue eyes that own every part of me appear before my hazy vision.

"Oh, Coop," she whispers, her hand going to my jaw. "It's been a horrible day for us all."

That's a fucking understatement.

"Beck still in our bed?" I ask, my voice unrecognizable even to my own ears.

"Yes, breathing and alive, thanks to you."

I grunt and take another swig from the crystal bottle.

"Don't do this to yourself."

"Do what, Kayla? Accept defeat? Accept the fact that I failed to do the one thing I always promised to do for this town and our children?"

"You didn't fail," she counters. "All of those kids are alive right now and in their beds because of you and everyone else who broke into that school."

I shake my head. "It should have never happened. I should have prevented it. There was a fucking helicopter on the goddamn roof that no one saw."

"Exactly. *No one* saw it. They could have landed it in the middle of the night for all we know. None of that matters anymore."

"It fucking matters."

"No, it doesn't! What matters is Julia is going

78

to be okay and all of our kids are alive. *That's what matters and that's what we need to focus on.*"

I drop my head, teeth grinding as I try to shake this unrelenting guilt that's claiming me.

"Look at me." Kayla frames my face, forcing my eyes to her. "You cannot prevent the evil that walks this earth, that is not on you. But you can prevent them from hurting others and you did that today. You're good at your job, Cooper. The best, just like you're the best father. And a pretty decent husband, I guess."

A rough chuckle shoves from my throat.

Even when she's sad, she's sassy.

She wraps her arms around my neck, bringing her pretty face an inch from mine. "You're the best man I know, and you'll always be this town's, and our family's, hero. Never doubt yourself or our faith in you."

I'm not entirely sure I deserve that faith but I'm done talking about it. Reeling her in, I close the distance between our mouths and take what has always belonged to me.

Afterward, she sits on the step below me and curls into my shirtless chest. "Give me some of that." She grabs the bottle from my hand and takes an impressive swig.

Minutes later, we move inside and crawl into bed with our children, my chest seizing up again as I stare down at my son, remembering how close I came to losing him today. A boy who put his terror aside to try and protect his aunt. One who tells me every day that he wants to be a cop and catch the bad guys.

I'm proud to call him mine, and I will fight until my last fucking breath to ensure the safety of my family and this town.

EPILOGUE

Julia

Two weeks later

"I'll bet you're more than ready to go home and be with your family," Nurse Betty says, taking the last of the release forms from me.

"I most certainly am, but I appreciate everything you all have done for me here. Thank you."

Her smile is kind as she rests her hand on my shoulder. "It was our pleasure, honey. You have a good man there," she says, her eyes shifting over to Jax.

Warmth invades my heart as I gaze back at my husband. He leans against the wall, his fierce eyes penetrating my soul.

"I do. He's my best friend," I tell her, my voice soft.

Our lives were flipped upside down and irrevocably changed two weeks ago. There's no way I would have gotten through it without him. He didn't leave my side once and has been caring, attentive, and overbearing…but in the best way.

A lot of Annabelle's days have been spent here with us and nights with Anna and Logan. I know he must miss our daughter as much as I do. No matter how many times I told him he could leave, he refused. We're both ready to be home and move on with our lives.

A knock on the open hospital room door grabs my attention. Surprise flares inside of me to see it's Ryder. "Ryder, hi."

"Hey, Julia…Jaxson." He reaches for Jax's hand, shaking it.

The nurse excuses herself, leaving us in privacy.

"I'm glad I caught you guys before you left. There's someone who wants to say good-bye to you." He waves for that someone to come in and my breath stalls at the sight of Connor and his mother.

"Connor," his name escapes me on a whisper. I've been asking about him constantly but no one would tell us anything except that he was safe.

"Hi, Mrs. Reid," he greets me, shifting nervously from foot to foot. The uncertainty in his eyes tugs at my heavy heart.

Carefully, I scoot just a little closer to the edge

of the bed and open my arms for him. "Come here."

He doesn't hesitate walking into my embrace, his arms gentle from where I had surgery.

"I'm so glad you're here. I've been worried about you."

"He's been worried about you, too," his mother says. "He feels really bad about what happened. We both do."

Releasing him, I lift his small handsome face to mine. "I'm going to be just fine. What happened is not your fault or your mom's. It's no one's fault but the bad guys. Understand?"

He nods but looks unconvinced.

A lot of guilt has been going around but all the wrong people have been shouldering it, especially my husband. It's in his eyes every time he looks at me. We've talked about it a lot but I know it's going to take time for all of us to get over what happened.

"Now what's this you've come to say good-bye?"

Biting his lip, he directs a hesitant look over at Ryder.

"Connor and his mother are being put into witness protection," he explains. "Until we're certain the threat against them is over."

Sadness grips me to know I won't get to see him anymore but I had a feeling this would happen. "I guess I'm not allowed to know where?" I ask.

Ryder shakes his head. "Sorry."

"I understand." I look back at Connor, my hand moving to his small cheek. "I'll miss you but what's most important is your safety, and I have no doubt that Agent Jameson will make sure you and your mom are well taken care of."

"Thanks for being so nice to me," he says. "Maybe one day I'll be able to come back."

"I hope so. I'd really like that."

He gives me one more hug then joins Ryder and his mother at the door.

"Thank you for being so good to both of us," his mother says.

I nod and offer her the best smile I can manage without bursting into tears. It isn't until I get one last wave from Connor that the dam breaks.

Jax pushes from the wall and comes to sit next to me, pulling me into his arms. "He'll be okay, Jules. Ryder will make sure of it."

"I hate that they have to hide like this."

"I know, baby." His hand coasts up and down my back, bringing me a comfort only he can.

I tilt my face up to his. He wipes my tears

away and drops a kiss to my forehead.

My favorite kind of kiss.

"You ready to get the hell out of here, Mrs. Reid?"

Even after all this time, my heart still skips a beat when he calls me that. "More than ready."

At precisely that moment the nurse walks back in, pushing a wheelchair. "I just saw your company leave and figured I'd bring this by."

"The wheelchair isn't necessary," Jaxson says, climbing to his feet. "I'll be carrying her out."

"Actually, as long as I move slow, I can walk," I tell them.

The nurse shakes her head. "Sorry, but it's hospital policy. You have to leave in the wheelchair. But once you're outside, your handsome husband can sweep you off your feet."

Smiling, she pushes the chair closer but Jax steps in front of it.

"The only way my wife is leaving this hospital is in my arms."

"Jax," I start, but he doesn't let me speak, his attention remaining on the nurse.

"Listen, there was a time I didn't think I'd ever get the chance to hold her again, let alone carry her, and I'm not going to let anyone take that privilege from me now. Policy or not."

My heart aches at the sorrow in his voice. It brings me back to the time years ago when we thought we lost each other forever because of Wyatt. It took so long to heal from that, and I fear this is going to take even longer.

"I tell you what," Nurse Betty says. "I'm going to leave this wheelchair here for you. If you choose not to use it I'll have no idea because I'm headed for my break." Her lips curve into a kind smile. "I wish you both the best."

I barely get the chance to thank her again before she walks out. Jax turns to me, not looking the least bit apologetic, but I didn't expect him to.

"Well," I say, lifting my arms. "Are you going to whisk me off into the sunset?"

Bending down, he scoops me up into his arms. "Yeah, and I plan to never let go."

Smiling, I press a kiss to his jaw and rest my head on his shoulder, relishing in what it feels like to be his.

The afternoon sun feels like heaven on my skin as we walk outside. He's careful as he deposits me into his truck and is even more cautious on the drive home, avoiding every pothole and bump.

My pain is minimal thanks to the medication they have me on. The only downfall is it makes me sleepy, but right now I am too eager to finally be home and reunited with our daughter to feel anything but excitement.

The moment we pull up to our house, Annabelle tears out the front door, a beautiful smile on her sweet face.

"Mama, Daddy!"

Jaxson exits the truck quickly and scoops her up into his arms. They share a moment before he carries her over to me, my passenger door already open and waiting.

He bends down close enough for Annabelle to hug me.

"Hi, my sweet girl," I greet her, a fierce ache building in my throat at the feel of her arms around my neck. It doesn't matter that I just felt them last night, not when I thought there was a time I'd never feel them again.

"I'm so glad you're finally home, Mama," she whispers.

"Me too."

Leaning back, she smiles at me. "Grams is inside. We have a surprise for you."

"You do?"

She nods excitedly. "Come and see."

Jaxson places her back on her feet. "You go ahead. We'll be right behind you."

As she dashes back up the porch steps, Jax lifts me into his arms again. I don't bother refusing, knowing it won't make a difference. And if I'm being honest, even though I'm more than capable of walking, I'll take my husband's arms any day.

There's lots of movement and shushes behind the screen door as he climbs the steps. Once we step inside, confetti is thrown at us.

"Surprise!"

My front entrance is filled with all of our favorite people. From the family we share land with to Anna and Logan and Grams. The children hold up welcome home signs and balloons, excited smiles lighting up their small faces. It makes my heart swell with love.

"What a welcome home this is."

"Do you love it, Mama?" Annabelle asks.

"I more than love it. Thank you."

Grams walks over to plant a kiss on my cheek, making Jaxson have to bend down. "Glad you're finally home, honey." Her worn hands frame my face, hands that have always given me love and comfort.

"Thanks, Grams. Me too."

"Come on in, lunch is in the kitchen," Grace announces, leading the way.

My kitchen island is filled with enough food

to feed an army. From sandwiches to fruit and veggie trays, salads, and of course, pies.

"Wow, you really outdid yourselves. This looks wonderful."

"Thanks, I slaved all morning," Sawyer says.

The ridiculous lie has us all bursting into laughter.

"Sampled is more like it," Grace returns with a huff.

Jax deposits me at the head of the table where balloons have been wrapped around a chair. The moment he steps back, Annabelle, Mia, and Hope crowd around me.

"We made you some presents," Mia says, handing me a gift bag.

"You girls are so sweet. You didn't have to do that."

"We wanted to and it was so much fun," Hope says.

Intrigued, I reach in and pull out a beautiful ceramic box that's been hand painted.

"That one is from me," Annabelle says. "It's a jewelry box."

"You made this?"

"Yep. Alissa took us to the new pottery place. It's so fun, Mama. We have to go again some-time."

"We definitely will."

Reaching back into the bag, I pull out a ceramic pie. My gaze shifts to Hope, a smile curling my lips. "I'm gonna guess you made this one."

She nods proudly. "I call it Angel Pie. Because you were our angel when we needed one."

Emotion burns the back of my throat as tears sting my eyes. Little do they know, all of them were my angels. Without them, I wouldn't have been as strong and calm as I needed to be.

"Thank you, sweet Hope," I say, trailing a finger down her small cheek.

"You're welcome."

"Open mine now," Mia says, excitedly.

Sniffling, I gather my composure and pull out the last ceramic painting to see it's a horseshoe. The messy colors running into each other has my heart swelling with love.

"This is beautiful, Mia."

"It's for good luck," she says.

"Thank you so much, girls. I'll treasure these forever."

We share a group hug, their little arms tangled around me. Parker and Beckett come over next, carrying a large glass vase filled with wild flowers.

"We got you these," Beckett says, placing them on the table in front of me.

"They're so pretty."

"They even picked them," Kayla adds.

"Here's the card." Parker thrusts an envelope at me, his eagerness putting me on alert.

My eyes shift to Grace and she gives me a subtle nod. I brace myself as I open it but still yelp when a leaping plastic frog jumps out.

Parker doubles over in laughter, Beck chuckling along with him.

"Boys!" I try to use my best scolding voice but end up laughing with them.

"Got ya good, didn't we?" Parker says.

"You did. I deserve a big hug for that one."

They don't hesitate. Their arms hug me tight, and I even receive a kiss on the cheek from Parker.

"We're glad you're back, Aunt Julia," Beckett says. The amusement that was in his voice moments ago is now gone.

"Thank you. You both are such brave boys." I want to say more but don't want to ruin the beautiful moment with the horrid memory we all wish to forget.

"All right, let's get Auntie Julia some lunch," Kayla says. "All of the kids go out to the deck, your plates are there. And by kids, I mean the big ones, too," she adds, eyeing all the men.

"I'll babysit," Grams chuckles, following them

out the patio door.

After bringing me a plate of food, the girls fix themselves one then join me at the table.

"You girls are amazing. Thank you for doing this."

"There are some casseroles and pies in your freezer, too," Grace says. "We didn't want y'all worrying about suppers while you're still tryin' to heal."

Their loyalty and friendship never cease to amaze me. "Thanks. That will be extremely helpful. I'm still having a hard time getting around."

"Did the doctor say how long before you're a hundred percent?" Anna asks.

"He figures about six weeks but we'll see. Every day is better."

At least for my body, the heaviness in my heart will take much longer to heal.

My gaze shifts outside to the deck where Annabelle sits on Jax's lap, eating her lunch. "How has she been sleeping?" I ask, looking back at Anna. The love she and Logan have shown my daughter is something I will never be able to repay.

"Better than the first week. She still tosses and turns. I think it will be better now that you guys are home."

"Mia is still sleeping with us," Faith confesses, her sadness mirroring the one in my chest. The memory of that horrible man pointing the gun in her face has panic gripping me all over again.

"Hope hasn't left Sawyer's side," Grace shares, her voice wavering with emotion. "She's even been going with him to the gym instead of the bakery with me, and her night terrors are horrible. She wakes up screaming at least once a night."

"And Parker?" I ask.

She wipes her tear-stained cheeks with her napkin. "He tries to hide behind his pranks but I sense his anxiety. He's more watchful and uncertain to go places. He's even asked Sawyer to teach him how to shoot."

"Beckett, too," Kayla says. "I also found a walkie-talkie in his room that leads to Parker. He told me it's so they can be prepared if the bad guys come back."

The pain in her voice has me reaching for her hand. "We'll get through this. We all will, it's just going to take time."

"I actually have an idea I want to run by you all," Anna says, bringing our attention over to her. "What would you think if I offered a group counseling session at the center for all the children? I could get it funded and run a few classes a week. That way we can offer it to all the families that were affected. I have a wonderful psychologist who deals with my veterans for PTSD. Of course I'll sit in on it too, since child psychology is my major."

"I think that's a fantastic idea," I say, meaning it.

"Me too," Faith agrees.

Grace and Kayla nod.

"Good. Then I'll get the details ironed out and we'll start as soon as possible. Any word on when they plan to reopen the school?"

"I'm not sure they will," I say, "not with only a few more weeks left in the school year. Besides, last I heard they're still trying to find a principal."

"It's too soon anyway," Kayla says. "They aren't ready to go back and neither am I."

I fear none of us will be ready to take that step, but I know the time will come when we need to. We have to in order to move on with our lives.

As we near the end of our lunch, I attempt to stifle a yawn but the pain medication has finally caught up to me.

Within seconds, Jax is by my side, lifting me into his arms. "Time for bed."

"I'm still good for a bit, Jax," I assure him, not wanting to be rude and leave my guests.

"You go." Faith nods. "We're just going to clean up then head out."

"Are you sure?"

"Yes, now go," Kayla orders, waving us away. "Let Hulk take you out of here before things go smash."

Us girls chuckle while Jaxson remains less than amused.

Kayla shrugs at his glare. "Sorry, Hulk, the opportunity presented itself and I couldn't pass it up."

Jaxson grunts at the apology and starts out of the kitchen.

I wave at my friends over his shoulder. "Thanks again, ladies. Tell the kids I love them."

"You bet. We'll come back tomorrow to check on ya," Grace yells, her voice trailing out of the room.

There's no slowing down my husband, he's a man on a mission. Wrapping my arms around his neck, I smile up at him. "How did you know I needed rest? Were you watching me?" I tease.

"I'm always watching you, Julia."

My heart tumbles in my chest, the sweet words warming my soul. I rest my head on his shoulder, my eyes growing heavy.

He lays me down and covers me with the blanket at the end of our bed. I wait for my kiss before he leaves but he surprises me by crawling in behind me, his body curling around mine.

Moaning, I snuggle back against him, relishing in the heat of his hard body.

"It's been way too fucking long since I held you like this," he murmurs, his lips pressing against the base of my throat.

"Way too long," I agree.

The hospital bed was not big enough for both of us. Jax was left to sleep on a terrible cot. I hated it but he reminded me that he had slept in far worse places and assured me he'd be fine. I'm glad that from now on I'll be feeling him next to me as I sleep. His arms have always been my sanctuary.

The sound of a light pitter-patter enters our room. I smile, already knowing whose small feet they belong to.

Jaxson twists his head, looking over his shoulder. "Come on up, baby."

Annabelle happily crawls in on the other side of me and moves in close, her sweet face only inches from mine. There are dark circles under her eyes, proving how hard the last couple of weeks have been for her.

"How did you like staying with Anna and Logan?" I ask, brushing a piece of hair out of her face.

She shrugs. "It was good. They took me out to do a lot of fun things but I'm glad it's just us again. I missed our family."

"I missed it, too," I admit on a whisper.

"Things are going to be better, Annabelle," Jaxson assures her. "I promise nothing will ever hurt our family again." There's more than a conviction in his voice, there's a threat and a promise.

"I know, Daddy, because you're my hero."

My heart melts into a giant puddle.

Jaxson reaches over me, his fingers dancing along the side of her small face.

"And mine," I say, feeling the need to add that.

He drops a kiss on my shoulder, his lips lingering, offering more than words ever could.

Annabelle snuggles in closer, exhaustion weighing heavily on her. Jaxson's strong arm curls around the both of us, bringing us peace and safety.

Sleep tries to claim me but I fight it off, wanting to bask in this moment forever. To absorb their heartbeats and their love surrounding me.

As long as we have this—have each other—we have everything. Nothing or no one can taint something as precious as this because love will always drive out hate, even in the most devastating times.

Jaxson

A sound pulls me from sleep. My eyes snap open and I take in the dark room where Julia and Annabelle sleep next to me. Seconds pass before I realize my phone is vibrating.

The red numbers on the clock glow with the time, showing it's the middle of the night. Reaching for my cell, I look at the screen and see a long distance number displayed.

My body tightens with anticipation, hoping it's the call I've been waiting for. Carefully, I climb from bed, trying not to wake my family.

My steps are quiet as I head into my office. "Yeah?" I answer, keeping my voice low.

"It's been done."

My eyes close, revenge seeping into my bleeding soul. "You sure you got them all?"

"Trust me, my brothers and I don't leave loose ends. Every single one you asked for has been terminated."

Meaning no women or children.

"Good. Thanks again. I would have done it myself but I can't leave my family."

"Don't worry about it. I'm glad we could return the favor you did for our father. Let us know if you ever need anything else."

"Same to you."

Ending the call, I send a text message to both Sawyer and Cade: *I just got word from Justice Creed. It's been done.*

I wait for some kind of remorse to hit me but I feel none. They deserved to pay for what they did, for what they almost took from me. When it comes to my family, I'll stop at nothing to keep them safe and ensure it stays that way.

I'm surprised when my phone dings back seconds later.

Sawyer: *I knew Thatcher would come through for us. May those motherfuckers rot in hell.*

Cade doesn't respond but I didn't expect him to. Pocketing my phone, I walk out of my office and back into my bedroom to find Julia stirring awake.

"Jax?" she whispers.

"Sorry, baby. I didn't mean to wake you."

"Who was on the phone at this hour?"

"No one for you to worry about."

Thankfully, she trusts me enough to accept that answer. "Come here," she says, reaching out for me in the dark.

Taking her hand, I climb in next to her, gathering her into my arms.

"You okay?" she asks, reaching up to touch the side of my face.

"I am now."

A smile stretches across her pretty lips. "Have I ever told you how much I love you?"

A shift happens deep within me, just like it always does when she says those words to me. Words that used to terrify me to hear, now the only fear I feel is to never hear them again.

"I think you have a time or two."

Her soft chuckle floats through the air. "Good, because I do. I have since I was seventeen years old and I'll love you until the end of time."

"I love you too, Jules. Always and forever."

She presses her lips against one of the deep, jagged scars on my chest, healing it more than time ever has and ever could.

That night I was finally able to rest easy, knowing justice had been served. Everyone who attempted to take what's mine is now burning in hell for an eternity, and anyone stupid enough to fuck with my family again will join them.

Until my dying breath, I will protect what's mine.

The End

For what's to come, please check out my website
www.authorkclynn.com

Acknowledgements

I'm blessed to have so many amazing people who love and support me in this beautiful journey I'm on. Most of them have been with me from the very beginning. They've had my back, believed in me, and wouldn't let me give up when times were daunting.

To everyone who has been a part of this with me—family, my beautiful editor, betas, friends, my author groups, bloggers, and readers around the world. You know who you are. Thank you. I love and cherish every single one of you.

Author Bio

K.C. Lynn is a small town girl living in Western Canada. She grew up in a family of four children—two sisters and a brother. Her mother was the lady who baked homemade goods for everyone on the street and her father was a respected man who worked in the RCMP. He's since retired and now works for the criminal justice system. This being one of the things that inspires K.C. to write romantic suspense about the trials and triumphs of our heroes.

K.C. married her high school sweetheart and they started a big family of their own—two adorable girls and a set of handsome twin boys. They still reside in the same small town but K.C.'s heart has always longed for the south, where everyone says 'y'all' and eats biscuits and gravy for breakfast.

It was her love for romance books that gave K.C. the courage to sit down and write her own novel. It was then a beautiful world opened up and she found what she was meant to do…write.

When K.C.'s not spending time with her beautiful family she can be found in her writing cave, living in the fabulous minds of her characters and their stories.

Made in the USA
Middletown, DE
11 June 2017